S0-BID-571

★PHOTOGRAPHS AND PERCEPTIONS BY SAM BRECK★

Published by Willow Creek Press, P.O. Box 147, Minocqua, Wisconsin 54548

Design: Donnie Rubo

Photographs: The photographs were made in these places: Michigan–Blissfield, Byron, Chelsea, Dundee, Durand, East Jackson, Gregory, Marion, Milford, Perry, Saline, Shepherd, South Lyon, Stockbridge; Indiana–Angola, Atlanta, Arcadia, Bulter, Corunna, Glenwood, Hamilton, Markle, North Manchester, North Vernon, Sweetser, Waterloo; Illinois–Onarga, Sheldon; Ohio–Hayesville, Pettisville, St. Henry, Stryker, Wauseon; There's also one photograph from someplace in Kentucky.

Originally published in 1992 by Heartland Press, an imprint of NorthWord Press, Inc.

Original ISBN 1-55971-147-1

Library of Congress Cataloging-in-Publication Data

Breck, Samuel L., 1928-

[It's a small town]

It's a small town if- - / photographs and perceptions by Sam Breck

p. cm.

Originally published under the title: It's a small town. 1989.

ISBN 1-59543-242-6 (hardcover : alk. paper)

1. City and town life- -United States. 2. City and town life- -Middle West. 3. City and town life- -United States- -Pictorial works. 4. City and town life- -Middle West- -Middle West- -Pictorial works. 5. United States- -Social life and customs- -1971- 6. United States- -Social life and customs- -1971- - -Pictorial works. 7. Middle West- -Social life and customs. 8. Middle West- -Social life and customs- -Pictorial works. I. Title.

E169.Z82B74 2005

977'.009734- -dc22

2005020472

Printed in Canada

NORMAL

Introduction

They're writing obituaries for small towns.

The nation's heavy thinkers–the sociologists, psychologist, and assorted other -ologists–are doomsaying, predicting that the American small town is a goner. We'd better act soon, they imply, and use some government money to preserve our towns in museums.

If it comes to that, I'll suggest putting a small town on the Mall outside the Smithsonian, where the politicians and social engineers, whose vision of small-town life comes from flying 30,000 feet overhead, will be reminded that a lot of the country's real strength is found in its little communities. In fact, the Inaugural Parade might be re-routed down the town's Main Street, right past the Dari-Dip store and the Koin Kleen laundromat.

Don't believe the folks with letters after their names. The small town is as alive as any place. It simply lacks the exhaust, the noise, and the squeeze-and-shove lifestyles that are epidemic in larger places. Just because there's no interstate exit at it's door doesn't mean a town is ready to be donated to the archaeologist. In fact, its isolation probably ensures its health. Chamber of Commerce types may harrumph at this notion, but they're followers of the dogma that change and congestion are always better and "good for the economy." What else would you expect from people who think only of super-somethings and high-tech industrial parks? What's good for *people* doesn't seem to concern them.

Admittedly, I'm addicted to little places, and although you may not be a terminal case like me, just the fact that you're holding this book indicates that you probably have a touch of envy, nostalgia, or curiosity about small towns. You probably also understand that the towns don't all look alike. If you're doubtful, visit a few each year and, in time, you'll be able to actually see small towns, not just look at them. You'll discover those delightful idiosyncrasies that make small places interesting and different. If you give it a sincere try, you may even find them fascinating.

So, angle-park your car on Main in front of the Western Auto, and take a slow-paced stroll down to the corner of Depot, then hang a left, cross the tracks to Mill, double back on Maple, Madison, Church, and School. Keep listening as well as looking. Small towns have a sound all their own. The sounds of tractors and trains. Tires on wet brick streets. And soft speech:

"Howdy."

"Mornin', Don."

"Hope you'll be at the Guild on Wednesday, Louise."

"See my dad's new Chevy?"

"Come back and see us again, ya hear? And have a nice day."

...If *from where it begins, you can see where it ends.*

. . . **If** *visitors are always asking, "What's there to do around here, anyhow?"*

HAMILTON
CHURCH OF
CHRIST

HAMILTON
UNITED
METHODIST
CHURCH

HAMILTON
WESLEYAN
CHURCH

GRANGE
#2109

HAMILTON
LIONS CLUB

HAMILTON
CLUB

OTSEGO LODGE
#403 O.E.S.

KNIGHTS
OF PYTHIAS
LODGE #228

HAMILTON
TEMPLE #51
PYTHIAN
SISTERS

HAMILTON
REBEKAH
LODGE #315

GAMMA KAPPA
CHAPTER OF
KAPPA
DELTA PHI

PSI RHO
CHAPTER OF
KAPPA
DELTA PHI

546 FLA

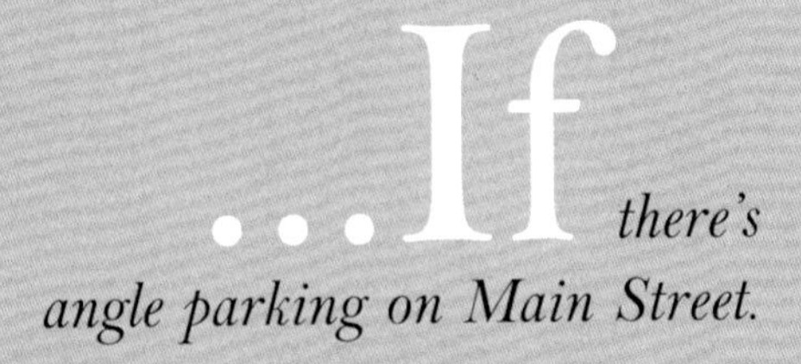

...If there's angle parking on Main Street.

. . . If *the well-worn joke about the cemetery is, "We don't need a fence around it, 'cause nobody wants to get in and for sure nobody's gettin' out."*

KECK

Blissfield
CIRCA 1824
49228

...If*, at first look, the Zip Code seems the only thing unique about the place.*

...If *there's always a wreath at the base of the war monument.*

MONUMENT
AND
MARKER
SALES DISPLAY
PH. 429-7098

...If *the selection isn't so great, but the service brings you back.*

. . . If *the bank closes early on Wednesday or Thursday afternoon.*

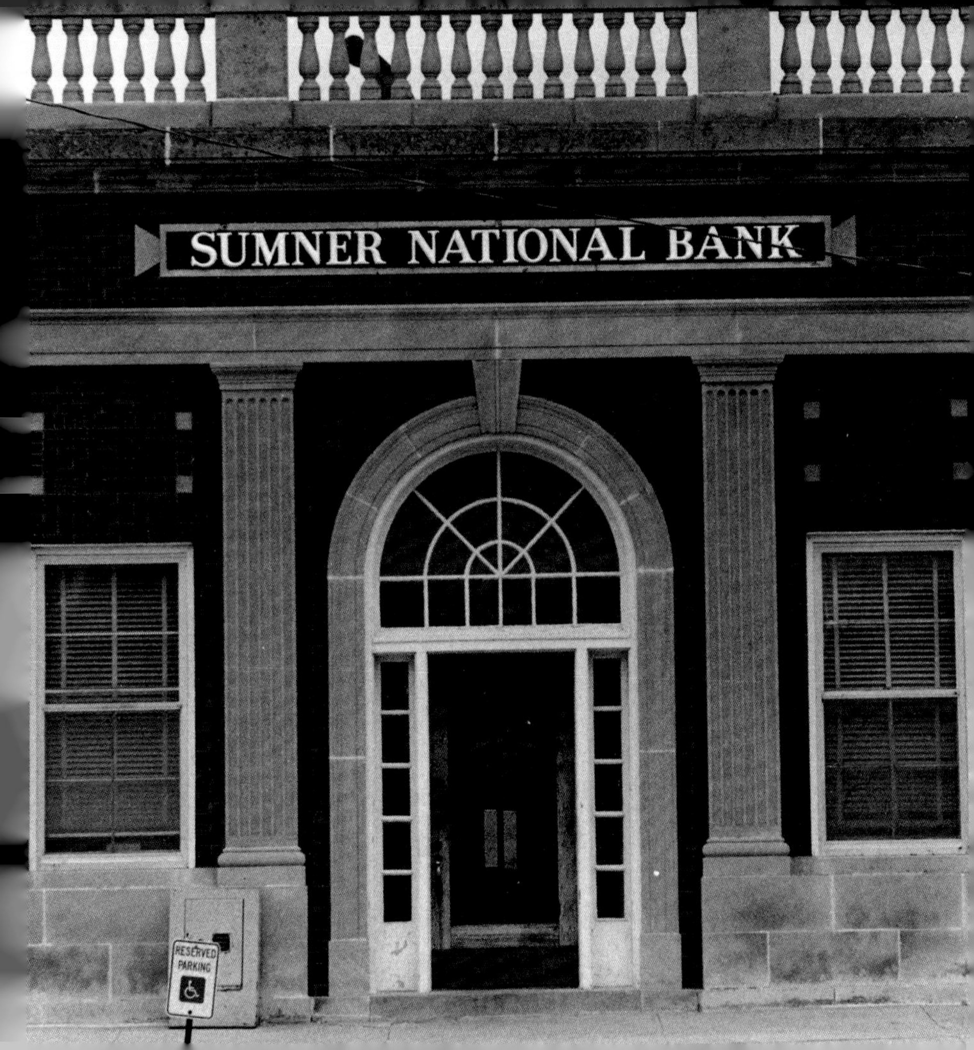
SUMNER NATIONAL BANK
RESERVED
PARKING

BEER
EAT

...If *the signs are more functional than promotional.*

. . . If *it's hard to get a date Wednesday evening because anyone you'd like to go out with has choir practice.*

...If *you don't have to feed a quarter to the air pump.*

. . . If *the motel room comes with a Gideon Bible and a flyswatter.*

PREPARE
TO MEET
THY GOD!

8-1858

MICHIGAN
MOTEL
THIS EXIT LEFT 1 MILE
3rd MOTEL

...If *lawn decor can be more competitive than attractive.*

...If *the old houses are called just that–not "landmarks" or "architecturally significant structures."*

DOROZO'S
CONGRATS
JOHN NEWMAN
JIM SIKORSKI

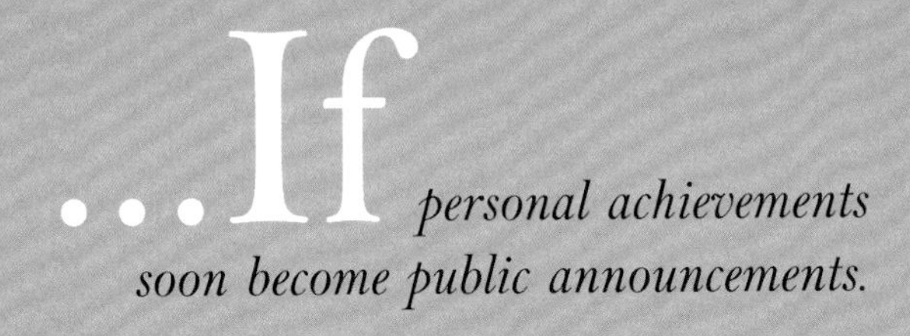

...If *personal achievements soon become public announcements.*

. . . If *the traffic signal at the main intersection is a blinker light.*

S. WASHINGTON ST.
E. FIRST ST.

...If *most of the streets are named for trees, presidents, compass directions, ordinal numbers, or members of your family.*

. . . **If** *the Legion or the VFW uses artillery as a lawn ornament.*

...If*, in the evening,*
you can hear a dog bark two blocks
away–and know whose dog it is.

...If *"the show" offers movies (not films) and is open only on weekends.*

FRISATSUN
COMING SOON

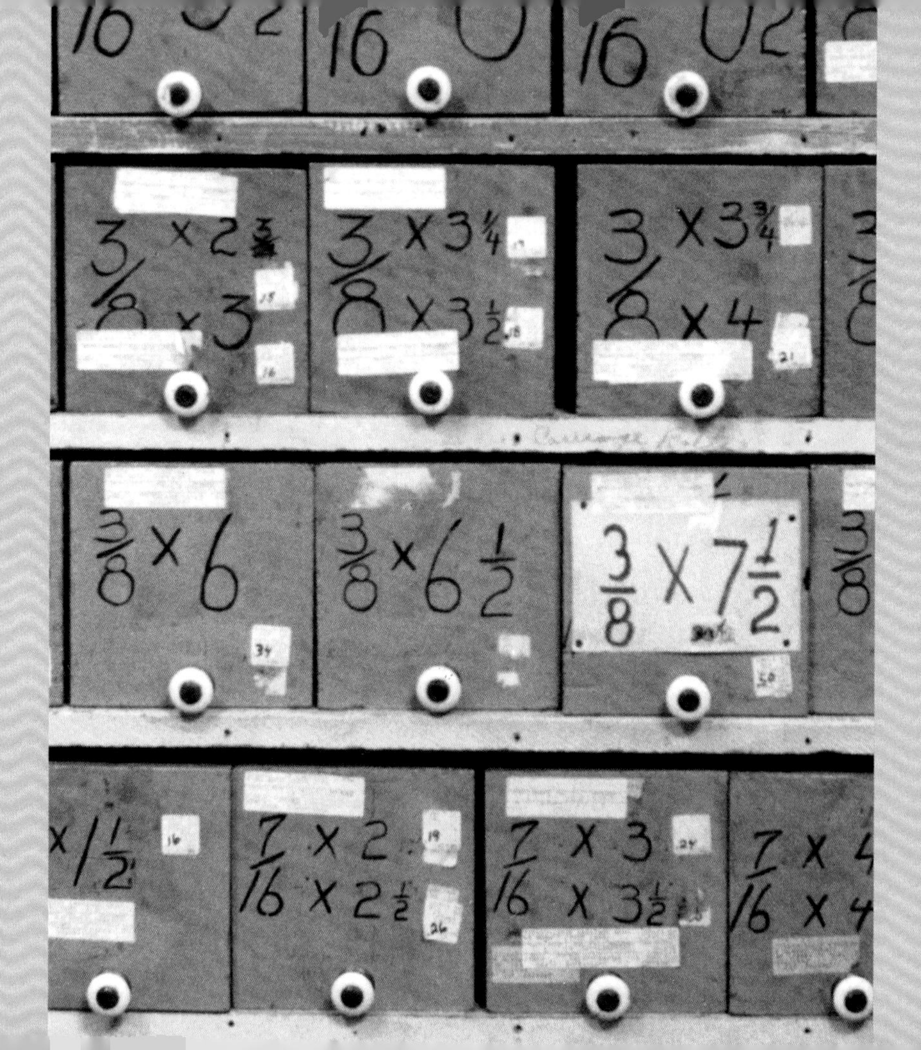

3/8 x 3 1/4
3/8 x 3 1/2
3/8 x 3 3/4
3/8 x 4
3/8 x 6
3/8 x 6 1/2
3/8 X 7 1/2
7/16 x 2
7/16 x 2 1/2
7/16 x 3
7/16 x 3 1/2

...If *the hardware store will sell you one bolt or one nut at a time.*

...If *a look at the waterworks is an essential part of the tour.*

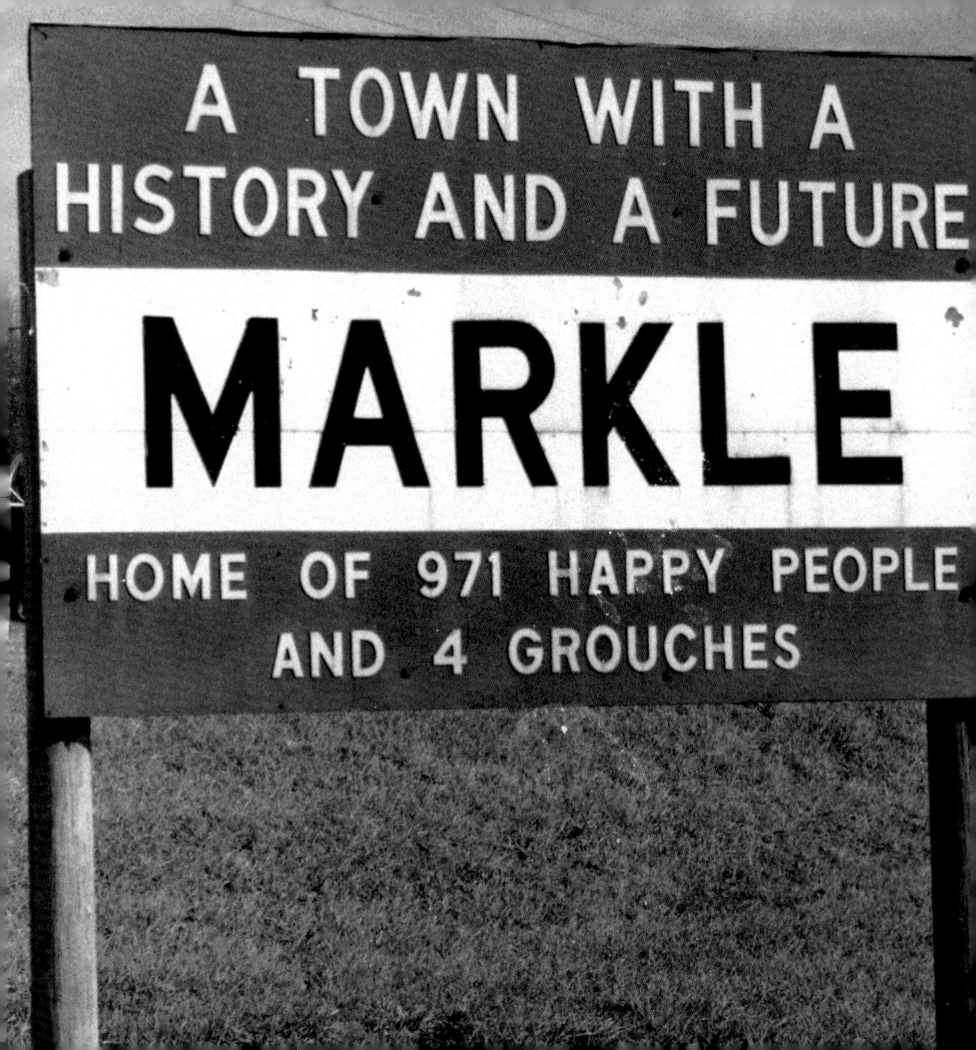

A TOWN WITH A
HISTORY AND A FUTURE

MARKLE

HOME OF 971 HAPPY PEOPLE
AND 4 GROUCHES

...If *the place doesn't take itself all that seriously.*

. . . If *there's not much to see, but what you overhear makes up for it.*

12 MIN. FOR EACH PENNY
1 HR. FOR EACH NICKEL
2 HRS FOR ONE DIME
INSERT COIN
TURN HANDLE TO RIGHT
AS FAR AS POSSIBLE
AFTER EACH COIN

...If *a penny buys some time on the meter.*

. . . If *the drive-in is owned by a neighbor, not managed by a computer in the next state.*

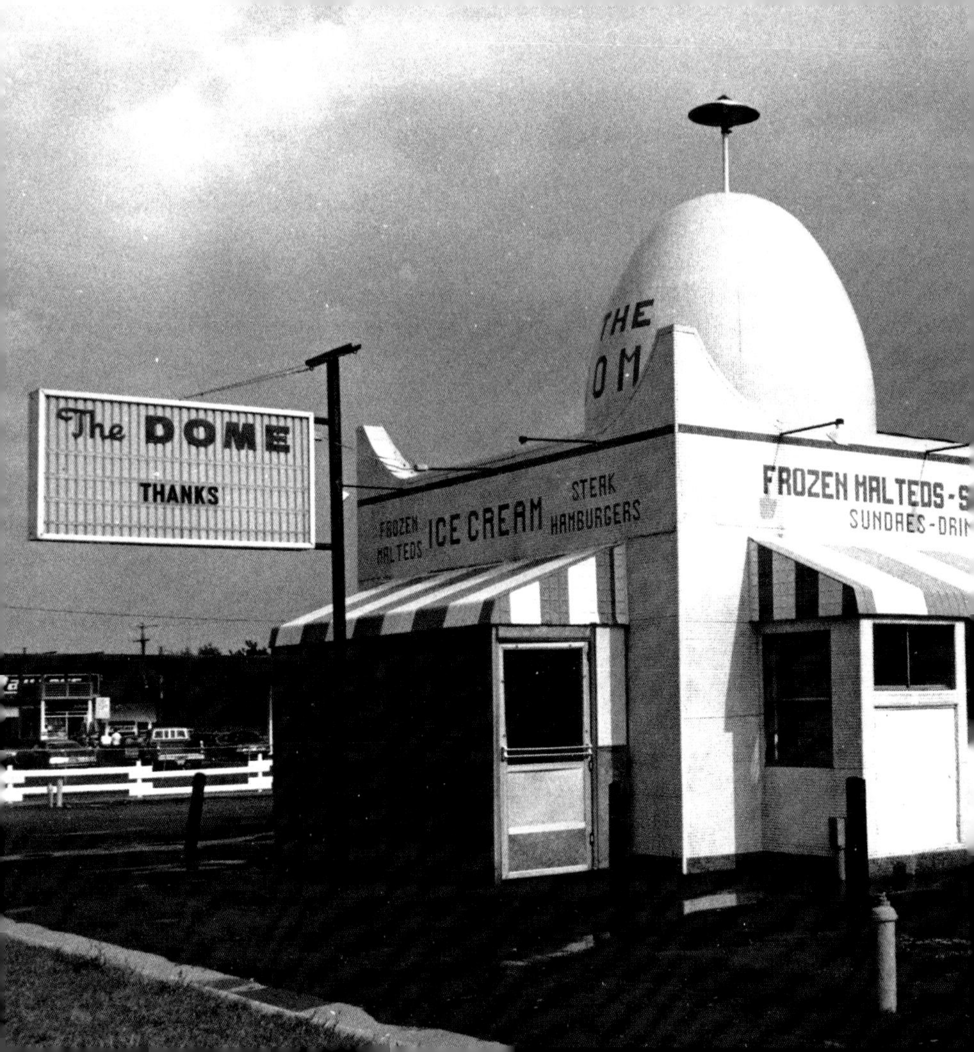

The DOME
THANKS
THE
FROZEN MALTEDS
ICE CREAM
STEAK HAMBURGERS
FROZEN MALTEDS

MAYOR'S
OFFICE

...If *government is accessible–and even friendly.*

. . . If *business can wait when it's time for dinner.*

CLOSED
FOR
LUNCH
WE SELL
PENNVERNON
WINDOW GLASS
STORE HOURS

FRANKS
BARBER
SHOP
Coke
Coca-Cola
AIR
FRANKS
BARBER
SHOP

...If *you get your hair cut (not "styled") in a one-chair shop where you can read* Sports Illustrated, Outdoor Life, *and* Popular Mechanics.

. . . If *, during the summer festival, the volunteer firefighters get thoroughly soaked–and so does everyone else.*

HOME OF THE
1980 CLASS C
BASEBALL STAT
CHAMPIONS

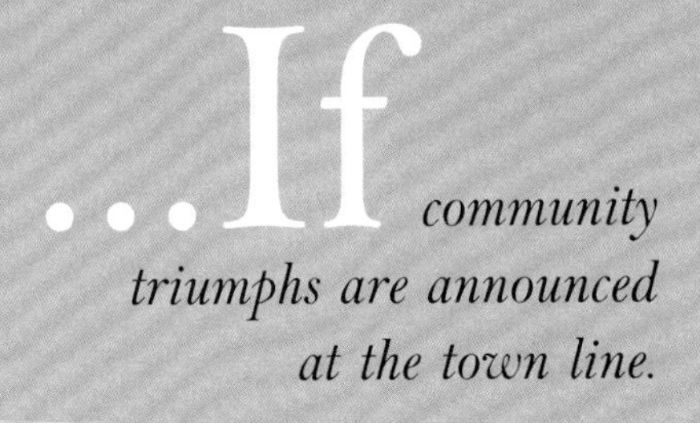
...If community
triumphs are announced
at the town line.

...If *folks think that growth is a good thing, but maybe it ought to wait until there are more folks in town to make it worthwhile.*

Buy Your
FAIR SEASON TICKETS
HERE

. . . If *you generally find split pea soup on Thursday's menu at the cafe, and Friday's special is likely to be tuna noodle casserole.*

...If *Sunday is what Sunday was.*

→ HOURS ←
TUE 10 TO 5
WED 10 TO 5
THUR 9 TO 5
FRI 9 TO 5
SAT 9 TO 4
SUN THE LORD'S DAY
Closed

...If *so many folks march in the parade that not many are left to watch it from the curb.*

. . . If *the IGA's downtown.*

MILLER'S
Holsum
Vitamin D
SELF-SERVE GROCERY
RIVERSIDE
WHOLESALE

...If *last Friday's high school game makes page one of this week's paper.*

...If *the train doesn't stop here anymore.*

. . . If *the Main Street clock isn't a digital clock.*

...If *the coolest, most delicious water anywhere comes from a constantly-bubbling fountain at the corner of Main and Maple.*

. . . If *the pay phone's got a rotary dial.*

South Lyon
Telephone Directory
Area Code 313
1985-86
(Issued November 1985)
AMERITECH
Michigan
Bell
Yellow
Pages

GULF

...If *you fill up on Friday or Saturday because the filling station's closed Sundays.*

. . . If *there's a cup with your name on it hanging in the cafe.*

NICKI
TRACY
BILL
DEBBIE
LARRY
GENE
WES
WES
LOUIE

863
GRAGE
SALE

. . . If *you saw stuff at last Saturdays's garage sale from your own sale two weeks ago.*

...If *you're from there and you're proud of the place–whatever its name may be.*

HELL